Raintree is an imprint of Capstone Global Library Limited, a company incorporated in England and Wales having its registered office at 264 Banbury Road, Oxford, OX2 7DY – Registered company number: 6695582

www.raintree.co.uk
myorders@raintree.co.uk

Designed by Aruna Rangarajan
Original illustrations © Capstone Global Library Limited 2020
Originated by Capstone Global Library Ltd
Printed and bound in India

ISBN 978 1 4747 7003 3
23 22 21 20 19
10 9 8 7 6 5 4 3 2 1

British Library Cataloguing in Publication Data
A full catalogue record for this book is available from the British Library.

Acknowledgements
We would like to thank the following for permission to reproduce photographs: Shutterstock: Color Brush, design element throughout, KRAUCHANKA HENADZ, design element throughout, Nikiparonak, design element throughout, PYRAMIS, 109, Theeradech Sanin, design element throughout.

Oil-Soaked Wings

by Emma Carlson Berne
illustrated by Erwin Madrid

raintree
a Capstone company — publishers for children

Dear Diary,

The past few months have been crazy, and not just because I moved across the country. I never thought we'd leave Chicago. The city had been my home my whole life. I loved the rumbling above-ground trains, the massive skyscrapers, the streets filled with people. . . Believe it or not, I even liked my school. It was the type of place where it was cool to be clever.

But then, when school ended for the year, Mum and Dad announced we were moving. They'd decided to leave their jobs as marine biologists at the Shedd Aquarium and move the whole family to Charleston, South Carolina! They both got jobs running somewhere called Seaside Sanctuary Marine Wildlife Refuge – jobs that were "too good to pass up", as they put it.

And at first, I couldn't believe Seaside Sanctuary would ever seem like home. Everything was different – the humidity, the salty air, the palmetto trees, the old brick streets lined with massive old oaks. Not to mention the flat, quiet beaches with water warm enough to swim in all year - you don't see that along Lake Michigan.

But it hasn't all been bad. For starters, I met my best friend, Olivia, on my first day at Seaside Sanctuary. She was sitting by the turtle pool, reading. By the end of the morning, I knew three very important things about Olivia:

1. Her older sister, Abby, is the vet at the sanctuary.
2. She doesn't like talking to people she doesn't know.
3. She wants to be a dolphin researcher when she grows up.

And I knew we were going to be best friends.

I still miss Chicago. But between helping the volunteers with feedings, cleaning tanks, showing tourists around and prepping seal food in the industrial-sized blender, I haven't had much time to think about my old life. And one thing is for sure - at Seaside Sanctuary, I'm never lonely, and I'm never bored.

Chapter 1

"Olivia!" I called down the beach. "Over here!"
I shook out my beach towel and spread it on white
sand as fine as baby powder.

In front of us, the ocean stretched out to the
horizon. When I first moved here to Charleston,
I had no idea an ocean could be so calm — or so
warm.

Olivia fussed with her towel, laying it out and
fidgeting with the edges until it was perfectly flat.

"I can't believe you found this place!" she said, finally lowering herself to her towel and closing her eyes against the sun.

"I know – it's like having our own private beach." I'd been on a hike the week before when I spotted a pathway near the end of a string of cottages not far from Seaside Sanctuary. I'd followed it through waist-high thickets of palmetto scrub before it ended on this totally deserted stretch of sand. You couldn't get to it from a street, which must be why it was deserted – and perfect for Olivia and me.

The day was perfect for the beach too – blue sky, blazing Charleston sun, a few puffy white clouds skating by. I lay on my back, closed my eyes and listened to the *shush-shushing* of the water. I inhaled the familiar salt smell – and something else. There was another smell today – something acrid.

I inhaled again and sat up. "Olivia, can you smell something weird?"

"No." She had her arm crooked over her eyes. Then she sat up too. "Yeah, actually." She sniffed. "It smells bad."

"I think it's the water." I got up and squatted down by the tide line. I touched the surface of the water with my fingers. My fingers came away coated with a brown film. "There's something on it."

I studied my fingers, rubbing them together. They felt greasy. Then, in an instant, I realized why, and my insides contracted. "It's oil."

Olivia gasped. "Oh no. Oil in the ocean is bad, no matter what."

I nodded. I might be new to coastal living, but even I knew that much. I shaded my eyes and gazed out to the flat horizon as if I might see some answers. But there was nothing.

"Elsa?" Olivia said behind me. "Look at that pelican."

I turned around. The large bird was squatting on the sand a few metres away from where we stood. But it wasn't the right colour for a pelican. Pelicans are usually a beautiful white-grey. This pelican was chocolate brown all over. It looked sick too.

I walked slowly towards it. "Hey, bird," I said softly. The pelican squawked and waddled away, but it didn't spread its wings and take off the way the bird normally would have. It didn't seem able to fly.

"Something's wrong with him." I squatted down and eyed the bird carefully. He had a big chunk missing out of the web on his right foot. But I wasn't focusing on his feet. It was his feathers that were the problem. "It's like he's covered in . . ."

I stopped and looked at Olivia. We realized at the same time what that something was.

"Oil," we both said at once.

Olivia and I quickly straightened back up.

"We have to tell someone," I said. "My parents. Or your sister." The first stirrings of panic were creeping up my chest. The dirty pelican squatted miserably on the sand. He looked sick. I felt sick when I looked at him.

"Can we take him with us?" Olivia asked. I knew just how she felt. I couldn't stand to see the sick, bewildered bird left all alone either.

"I don't see how," I told her. "We don't have any way to carry him. And I don't want to hurt him by accident if he struggles."

Olivia nodded. "You're right. Let's just go and get help and get back here — fast."

We packed up our towels and left the beach as quickly as we could. Just before we reached the head of the trail, I looked back at the deserted stretch of sand. The pelican still sat there, just above the tide line, the dark, filmy water lapping at its feet.

～

Something was wrong when we got back to Seaside Sanctuary – I could tell straight away. There were no volunteers scrubbing tanks or carrying buckets of fish to the animals. In fact, all of the paths and pens were deserted, except for the animals inside.

I stumbled over a broom in the middle of the centre path, lying there as if someone had dropped it suddenly. An overturned bucket lay beside it. Olivia and I looked at each other with wide eyes.

"Where is everyone?" she said, clearly as worried as I was.

I didn't have an answer. The place was eerily quiet. The only sounds were the hum of the air conditioner, the soft lapping of the ocean waves nearby, and the occasional squeak of our dolphins in their coastal sea pen.

Then I noticed my mum's red rucksack sitting outside the door to the office. She was here.

Olivia and I ran up and opened the door. Mum, Dad and Abby, Olivia's older sister and the sanctuary vet, turned around. A man I didn't recognize was there with them. Mum's face was pale, and my first thought was that an animal had died.

"Oh, Elsa, Olivia. We've had terrible news," Mum said.

"We saw something terrible too!" I burst out. "On the beach. There's a pelican covered in oil."

Mum's face grew even paler. "That's what I was trying to tell you," she said. "There's been an oil spill."

I gasped. Olivia grabbed my arm. Oil spills were a disaster – I knew that, even if I'd never actually been near one. Oil sometimes spilled out of a ship or an underwater pipeline, because of an accident of some kind. It would spew out onto the water and float on the surface. The oil would kill fish and crabs and coral and seaweed and dolphins and seals and birds. And it would stay and stay until someone cleaned it up, which was hard – and expensive – to do.

Dad put his arm around my shoulders. "This is Chris Hauser. He's a wildlife biologist with the Department of Wildlife and Fisheries. He came to give us the news. Apparently a tanker carrying oil had collided with another ship not far from shore. No one was hurt, but a huge hole was ripped in the side of the tanker. We can expect oil coming ashore here on Sullivan's Island within the next few hours."

"Dad, it's already here." Quickly, I detailed what Olivia and I had seen.

When I finished, the adults nodded. Their faces were lined with worry.

"Seaside Sanctuary has volunteered to be a cleaning station for oiled pelicans," Abby told us. "There are probably going to be hundreds affected by the spill, and they'll all need to be fed, watered, warmed up and cleaned before they can be released again. It's a big job, but as we're right on the coast we're the most logical option."

"What can we do to help?" I asked.

"Chris is going to advise us and work with us," Abby continued. "This afternoon, workers will set up a temporary building at the edge of the property. The Department of Wildlife and Fisheries will organize volunteers to work with the birds."

Chris nodded. He was a middle-aged man with the kind of rough skin that signalled years spent outdoors. "We're really grateful to Seaside Sanctuary for volunteering all your space and resources. We're going to need them."

He looked right at Olivia and me. "These pelicans will die without help — and they'll suffer. The oil will poison their skin, they'll swallow it when they try to preen their feathers, and then it will poison their insides. They can't keep warm with oil covering them, and they'll become too cold to live. They can't fly, so they can't hunt for fish. They'll starve."

"Stop!" I cried suddenly. I couldn't stand to hear that terrible list of sufferings. "We'll do everything we can! We'll clean them."

"Good." Mum squeezed my shoulder. "We're going to need every pair of hands we can find. The pelicans are depending on us."

I thought back to the sad, oiled bird on the beach. He needed us. They all did. I was so glad we could do something to help them.

Chapter 2

From there on out, everything was different.
Within two hours, I barely recognized Seaside
Sanctuary. Trucks started arriving, and workers
unloaded plywood and tarps and tubs and hoses
and cases and cases of what turned out to be
washing-up liquid.

Mum called a local fabric recycler and soon
a van pulled up and dumped what seemed like
a tonne of old towels. Everywhere I looked,

people were setting up tubs, connecting hoses, constructing crude tables and walls out of plywood and two-by-fours. Up on ladders, workers were stapling heavy-duty tarps to skeleton walls and carrying in rolls of chain-link to make pens.

Mr Hauser was in the middle of it all, directing workers, supervising the placing of the washing tubs. "We've got several stations," he explained to Olivia and me. "Follow me. I'll walk you through the process."

I appreciated that he talked to us as if we were grown-ups, which adults hardly ever did. Most of the time, they talked to us as if we were kids who had food on our faces. But Mr Hauser was a different kind of grown-up. I could see that.

"When the birds are first brought in, Abby will examine them," he explained. "Mostly, she's looking at their mouths, to see if they've swallowed too much oil, or to see if their skin is damaged from the oil. Then we'll put them in these pens." He pointed to the chain-link pens a worker was assembling. "There they'll be banded, so we can keep track of them. The first thing is we'll feed and water them."

"I thought the first thing would be to wash the oil off them," Olivia said.

Mr Hauser nodded. "Yes, that's what most people think. They will get washed. But remember, these birds haven't been able to eat because they can't hunt. And because their feathers are stuck together with oil, their bodies are losing moisture and getting dehydrated. The washing process is actually pretty traumatic for the birds. It's the physical equivalent of you or me running a marathon. They have to be strong to withstand it. And food and water will help with that."

"So then what?" I urged him. "After they eat

and drink and rest?"

Mr Hauser led us across the tarp enclosure to a long table that stretched almost the entire length of the temporary building. Plastic tubs were arranged along the top, on mats, with big numbers in front of them.

"Then they'll get washed," he continued. "This is the big moment for them. We'll hose them and carefully scrub their feet and skin. The volunteers will use cotton buds to get the oil out of the birds' eyes and mouths. Here, this way."

He led us outside the temporary building and over to another series of pens at the very edge of the sanctuary's property. The pens were open to the air, but the chain-link was blocked with plywood and white sheets hung over the entrances.

"Why are they blocked off?" Olivia asked.

"This is where the birds will go once they've

been cleaned," Mr Hauser said. He pushed open a gate. Inside was a large pool with Astroturf stapled over the edges. "They can rest here, preen their feathers, and let their natural oils coat them again. We'll feed them fish, *but* you have to stay behind the white curtains when we throw fish to them."

He held up a finger. "It's very important the pelicans don't start associating humans with food. We don't want them to get comfortable with us. In fact, as strange as it sounds, we almost want them to be a little *afraid* of us. That way they'll avoid humans after they're released. That's better for wild birds – to stay wild."

With that, Mr Hauser let the curtain drop, shielding the pen once again.

"Wow!" I exhaled. The whole process was a little overwhelming. "And then they're released?"

"And then they're released. Once they can

show us they're eating fish, we'll drive them out, away from the oil and let them go."

Olivia and I looked at each other. I don't think either of us had any idea how much work went into helping oiled birds. I'd just imagined that we'd bring them in, scrub them off and let them go.

Suddenly, we heard the *thunk-thunk* of van doors slamming out in the car park. Mr Hauser looked at his watch. "That's the first batch of pelicans now." He fixed us with a serious gaze. "Are you girls ready? This won't be an easy sight."

I took a deep breath and squared my shoulders. Olivia nodded firmly. "We're ready."

Chapter 3

Workers pulled crate after crate off the vans. They looked like dog crates, but each one held one or two or three oiled pelicans.

Dad had been glued to his phone the whole time we were talking to Mr Hauser, and now I realized why – already people were pulling up in the car park. I recognized some of our regular volunteers in the crowd, but there were new people too.

"Volunteers! Inside the washing tent, please!" Mum shouted from the doorway of the temporary building. She was juggling a pile of papers, her hair flying in her face, and seemed flustered. "Abby will lead a training session on washing techniques." She turned to the workers unloading the crates. "Put the pelican crates in a line by the admission pens," she said. "Mr Hauser, I need you in here, please."

With that, she disappeared into the building. Olivia and I looked at each other, then rushed after her. We found her inside, muttering to herself, her face flushed.

Mum looked up as we entered. "We really cannot do this all ourselves. The Department of Wildlife and Fisheries said they'll send more volunteers in the morning – trained in bird-washing – but in the meantime, we'll have to make do with this first batch. Girls, I want you to help transfer the oiled birds into the holding pens."

Olivia nodded. I swallowed hard. I hated to see sick animals, and these birds were very, very sick. Still, I had to be brave – we both did. These pelicans had no one else to depend on.

We opened the door to the first cage. A pelican sat towards the back, blinking at us in the sudden light. He was brown all over, just like the pelican on the beach. He didn't move as I reached in and gently scooped him towards me. A healthy bird would be squawking and flapping all over the place, trying to get away. It seemed like he was being gentle, but his quietness was a sign of how sick he really was.

Suddenly I stopped. The pelican had a chunk missing from the web of his right foot. "Olivia! It's the pelican from the beach – the one we first saw!"

Olivia gasped and looked at him more closely. "You're right. I'm so glad they picked him up."

"You're going to be OK, buddy," I murmured to him.

Olivia helped me carry the bird to the holding pens. We sometimes had pelicans at Seaside Sanctuary, so we knew how to hold one. Adults could carry the birds by themselves, but we were smaller, so we had to do it together. One of us gently held his beak closed, so he wouldn't snap at us, and the other held him firmly under one arm, his wings folded against his body. We didn't want him flapping around and hurting himself – or us.

We carried him to the row of admission pens. I could smell the oil on him. Normally pelicans mostly smell like fish, but this guy smelled like chemicals – like no animal should smell.

We placed him in the pen, where he waddled to the back and then just stood there, looking miserable. Gently, I closed the door behind him and latched it.

"I don't think I can do another one," I said. Before I could stop them, tears were spilling down my cheeks. Olivia hugged me. She was crying too. "It's just so awful seeing them this way," I sobbed.

She nodded and snuffled, wiping her nose. "But we have to keep going. They need us. They'll die without our help," she said.

I took a deep, wobbly breath and tried to stop crying. "I know." Suddenly anger swept over me, as fresh as the tears had been. "Who's responsible for this? That's what I want to know! These pelicans were just living their lives, swimming and fishing and flying, and all of a sudden, they're poisoned. Who did it? Who?"

By the end, I was practically yelling. I didn't know why I was shouting at Olivia. It wasn't her fault. She just happened to be standing there.

"It was two tankers that crashed into each other," Olivia said. "You remember what Mr Hauser said."

"Yeah, but somebody owns those tankers. We should find out whose fault it was," I said. "Companies pay to clean up oil after spills. Whoever did it this time is going to pay to help these birds and the beach and all the other animals they've hurt or killed."

Olivia nodded. "I know. I feel the same way. But that will have to wait. There are more birds coming off the vans. Come on."

The rest of the day was a blur of oiled pelicans, dog crates, bird bands, plywood, chain-link, buckets of fish, buckets of soap and hoses. Mum and Dad and Abby and Mr Hauser were everywhere, directing volunteers, showing vans where to park, banding birds as they were brought in.

Quietly, volunteers started a pile at the very edge of the property, behind the office: birds that had died on the journey from the beach. They had to be examined and counted too. All the numbers needed to be reported to the Department of Wildlife and Fisheries.

By early afternoon our hands were greasy and stained brown. My hair was a mess, and Olivia had brown streaks on her cheeks from where she'd pushed her hair back. But we didn't stop working. We couldn't stop – there were too many birds. I kept walking past the pen where we'd put that very first pelican. I was already thinking of him as ours.

"Olivia," I said, when we both stopped to rest outside his pen for a minute. "I think this guy deserves a name."

"You know what Abby always says . . ." Olivia began.

"I know, I know! 'Don't name them, you'll get too attached, they're wild animals, not pets,'" I repeated, quoting Abby. "But . . ."

I crouched down by the wire mesh and looked at the pelican. Abby had banded him number 563. He gazed back at me calmly. Birds can't show distress on their face, like mammals. They don't have facial expressions. But I could feel his desperation anyway.

"Pellie," Olivia said suddenly.

"What?" I looked up at her.

"Pellie. His name is Pellie." She stared at him. "And I don't care if we get attached. I *want* to get attached."

I nodded. "I like that. Pellie it is."

Finally the rush of birds slowed. As the sun was setting in a blaze of rose and gold, the last van slammed its doors and drove off, its tail lights glinting as it disappeared up the driveway.

The volunteers would all be back, bright and early, but the first day was finished.

"Phew." Mum exhaled as she sank down on an overturned bucket. She leaned over and rubbed her face. "What a day."

We all sat around her, covered in feathers and oil. The birds were quiet in their pens, a true sign of how sick they were. If they'd been healthy they would have been causing quite a ruckus, I knew. No one said much. I felt flattened by the sight of all the sick birds and hopeless at the thought of how many more were still out there.

"Come on, everyone!" a cheerful voice interrupted. I looked up to see Mr Hauser holding a tray with six steaming mugs balanced on it. "I hope you don't mind me taking over your kitchen briefly. I didn't want to disturb you." He handed around the mugs.

"Mmm," Mum inhaled. "Sassafras tea! Where did you get it? It's not from around here."

"No indeed." Mr Hauser took a noisy sip of his. "I'm not from Charleston originally. My family is from West Virginia, and my mother regularly sends me packets of roots she's collected around our house. Ginseng too."

I inhaled the sweet, liquorice-smelling steam and took a long sip. The scalding liquid burned a little path of fire right to my belly. "Mmm," I echoed.

"I thought we could all use a little pick-me-up," Mr Hauser continued. "I know the first day after a spill is hard. You can't help but feel knocked down. I always do. But I've seen a lot of spills, folks. These first few days are critical. And we're making progress. We saved dozens of birds today, and we'll save more tomorrow. We can be proud of that."

I looked around at Mum, Dad, Abby and

Olivia, all sipping their mugs of hot tea,
resting, getting strong for tomorrow, and I
saw small smiles creeping over their faces too.
Mr Hauser was right. We couldn't let ourselves
get discouraged yet. Not when we'd done so
much – and there was still so much left to do.

Chapter 4

When I opened my eyes the next morning and saw the fresh South Carolina sunshine washing over my walls, I threw my covers off so hard they fell onto the floor. Today was a new day, which meant there were new birds to help. I pulled on a fresh T-shirt and shorts and washed my face in cold water until my cheeks glowed.

In the kitchen, I found Mum making eggs and bacon. She set the steaming plateful in front of me. "I'm glad you're up," she said. "I heard from Chris Hauser early this morning. The Department of Wildlife and Fisheries is sending about fifty volunteers, all trained in oiled-bird rehabilitation. And we'll be accepting vans of birds all day. The sanctuary will be full by the end of the day, so we're all going to need our strength."

"Are we going to be taking in any of the birds permanently?" I pulled a stack of toast towards me and slathered butter on the first two slices.

Mum shook her head. "We're full. They'll either be released or sent to another facility further up the coast."

"Got it." I wolfed down the eggs and bacon, gulped a glass of milk and was down the steps with my toast before Mum had even sat down.

Olivia must have eaten faster than I had, because she was already waiting at the entrance to the tent when I arrived. Her face was excited.

"Pellie ate three fish!" she called as soon as she saw me.

"Yes!" I cheered, peering into his pen. He sat in the same position as the day before, looking miserable. But he was alive, and he'd eaten. That was something.

"And he had some water, so Abby says he's strong enough to be washed," Olivia said.

"How long have you been down here?" I asked, following her into the tent.

"Since dawn," she answered over her shoulder. "That's when they arrived too."

"Who's th—" I started to ask. But then I stopped in astonishment.

The tent was buzzing with activity. At least fifty people in matching blue T-shirts were filling tubs with water — some soapy, some clean — laying out brushes and swabs, and organizing piles of towels.

"Isn't it wonderful?" Olivia asked happily.

"The trained volunteers!" I said. "Yes! This is exactly what we need!"

"Are you girls the resident experts?" someone asked behind us.

I turned around. A no-nonsense looking woman stood behind us, holding an oiled pelican in her arms. Her hair was cut short, and her arms and hands looked strong and tanned.

"I don't know if we're experts, but we live here," I said. "I'm Elsa, and this is Olivia. Can we help?"

"Just what I was going to ask," the woman said, leading us over to one of the soapy tubs. "I want to show you girls how to wash the birds, so you can do the next one on your own. I'm Katie, by the way. I'm heading up the group of volunteers sent over by the Department of Wildlife and Fisheries."

"Are you a volunteer too?" I asked.

Katie nodded. "I am," she said. "I've been specially trained in cleaning oiled birds and other animals. My husband and I kayak year-round, so I've seen the devastation that oil spills can cause. I started volunteering with the washing squad five years ago, after I retired from teaching."

She put the pelican down on a towel and examined his leg band. "This one is number 563. Elsa, can you note that on this form?" She pointed to a clipboard resting nearby.

"That's Pellie!" Olivia exclaimed.

"You know this bird?" Katie asked.

I nodded. "We found him on the beach. We're really rooting for him."

Katie laughed. "Me too. Well, Pellie is a young male, about a year old. He's swallowed some oil — enough to make him sick but not enough to kill him."

She showed Olivia how to hold Pellie's body firmly on the towel, with his feet tucked underneath him and one hand on either side to hold down his powerful wings. "We don't want him flapping around and hurting himself," she explained. She opened his huge beak. The skin of the pouch below his beak stretched like a finely pleated accordion.

"Abby has already washed out his mouth, so he doesn't swallow more oil. But I'll give it a thorough pass again," Katie continued. She vigorously wiped Pellie's tongue and the inside of his beak with a torn-up towel square. "Now we'll get him in the water and get him cleaned up."

"Is washing him going to be hard on him?" I asked, remembering what Mr Hauser had said about the washing process being like a marathon.

Katie nodded. "It's an unnatural process for a wild animal. He's being closely handled by humans

— manhandled, really. That's one reason why it's so stressful. He won't like it, but it's a necessity. We have to get the oil off his feathers." She picked up Pellie and plunged him in a plastic tub of soapy water so he was submerged up to the bottom of his neck. "We use normal washing-up liquid to wash them," she said over the sound of Pellie splashing. "It's made to cut through oil, which is just what we need. Elsa, you hold Pellie's body. Olivia, you hold his beak." She moved us into position. "I'll scrub."

"Now, do you girls know why oil is so dangerous to bird feathers?" Katie asked, as she rubbed Pellie's chest and stomach.

"Ah . . ." I looked at Olivia. I knew that oil was dangerous to birds, but it occurred to me that I didn't know exactly *why*.

"Bird feathers are perfectly arranged so that they overlap each other, like tiles on a roof," Katie explained. "Each feather has little barbs that interlock with each other to create a seal. The pelicans — and all other birds — have what is basically a waterproof shell around their bodies twenty-four seven. They're warm and dry on the inside, because their feathers keep water and cold air on the outside." She carefully stretched out one of Pellie's massive wings. "You wash now, Elsa, OK? I'll hold."

I dipped a towel square into the soapy water and carefully rubbed the long, beautiful feathers. The oil came off in brown droplets.

"Birds spend a lot of time every day preening — that's cleaning and arranging their feathers — to maintain that waterproof seal," Katie went on. She stretched out Pellie's other wing and nodded at me to wash it.

"But the oil messes all that up," Olivia said, sounding as if she was guessing a bit.

"Right." Katie folded Pellie's other wing back

up and massaged soapy water up his neck. "Oil mats the feathers. The little barbs get separated, the feathers get disarranged and poof! The waterproof seal is gone. The bird is without his warm coat. He'll die pretty quickly of cold."

I shuddered. What a terrible way to die. I didn't even want to think about that happening.

Katie finished Pellie's neck. He was warm under my hands, but I could feel the tension in his body. He was terrified.

Moving quickly but carefully, Katie washed Pellie's head. She used a soapy cotton bud to clean every trace of oil out of his eyes and the nostrils at the top of his beak. Then she wrapped him up firmly in a dry towel.

"He's done!" she announced. "Now he needs to rest, dry out and preen his feathers back into place."

Olivia lifted Pellie's body in her arms, and I

gently held his beak closed. I could sense from his body how exhausted he was from the washing.

We made our way between the tubs and carried him gently to the rehab pens for washed birds. Katie pointed out which pen to put him in. There were already three other cleaned birds in there. I hoped Pellie wouldn't feel so scared with the other pelicans around.

"Get well," I whispered to Pellie.

Soon they'd drop the white curtain across the opening, and we wouldn't be allowed to see him any more.

I told myself that was for the best, and it really was. These were wild birds, not pets. It would be even more dangerous for them if they started getting used to humans. They needed to stay away for their own good.

But it didn't mean I wasn't sad that we'd only

get to see him with a curtain in the way.

"Will he be released soon?" Olivia asked Katie.

"He has to show us he can eat live fish first," Katie replied. "These birds have had a terrible shock. Their bodies have been badly damaged by the oil. Sometimes they just can't recover. If Pellie can't eat live fish, he won't be able to survive on his own."

"Well, if he can't, he can stay at Seaside Sanctuary," I said stubbornly. "We have pelicans here."

But I knew as well as Olivia did that we were at capacity with our pelicans. Mum had already made it clear that we wouldn't be taking in any of the oiled birds.

Besides, Pellie should be free. That's where he'd be happiest. He deserved to spend his days soaring over the ocean, not trapped behind chain-link fences. If he could just eat. He had to.

He just had to.

Chapter 5

Olivia and I were still in the tent when
Mr Hauser came looking for us. "I'm taking the
department's boat out to search for more oiled
birds," he said. "Do you girls want to come? I could
use some fast muscle behind the net."

"You catch them in a net?" I asked. "Doesn't
that hurt them?"

Mr Hauser shook his head. "No, it just
restrains them. They can't move much because

of the oil covering them, so there's no danger they'll thrash and hurt themselves. Interested in coming along?"

Olivia and I looked at each other. "Sure!" I said. "Let me tell my mum."

Mum had the office phone pressed against her ear and her mobile phone was ringing on the desk, so she just nodded and waved me out of the room when I told her we were going out on the boat with Mr Hauser. It was clear she had her hands full at the sanctuary.

We crammed ourselves into Mr Hauser's truck, which was full of empty pelican crates, bottles, nets and tools. The seats were covered in oily bird feathers.

Fifteen minutes of bouncing on rutted roads brought us to the beach where we'd first seen Pellie. But it looked different now. Black, stringy goop was washed up on the white sand. The mess stretched down the beach in both directions as far as I could see.

Olivia and I climbed slowly out of the van. Mr Hauser followed with an armful of white cloth and three nets with long handles.

"Is this the oil?" I asked slowly. It wasn't liquid like I thought it would be. It was solid and soft when I squatted down to touch it with the tips of my fingers.

"There's so much of it," Olivia said, sounding as if she might start crying. "It's ruining the whole beach."

Mr Hauser shook out the white cloth he was holding, which turned out to be the kind of zip-up jumpsuit I'd seen hazmat workers wear. "It's not just ruining the beach," he said. "It's poisoning it. A beach is its own ecosystem, and the oil affects all the life on it: birds; marine mammals; fish; land mammals; crustaceans such as crabs and shellfish; marine plant life such as seaweed; and land plant life such as grasses."

Looking at the spoiled white sand, I felt sick. "Is the company responsible going to clean it up?" I demanded angrily. I didn't mean to snap at Mr Hauser – I was just so angry. It felt like I needed *someone* to blame.

He handed me a net. "The authorities have been talking to Coastal Oil, the company whose tanker spilled. It turns out the captain of the tanker wasn't monitoring the sonar. That's why he collided with the other tanker. Coastal Oil said they'll pay for the clean-up, but we haven't seen much action at all. Just promises."

"That's awful! There should be workers out here right now, cleaning this up." I clenched my hands into fists.

"I agree," Mr Hauser said. "And I understand your anger. I feel the same way when I see this beautiful, delicate ecosystem being destroyed. But right now, there are still pelicans out there that need our help. Are you girls ready to go in the boat?"

I'd been so focused on the oil – and my anger – that I hadn't noticed a small, battered motorboat tied up to a dock just down the beach. The words *State of South Carolina Department of Wildlife and Fisheries* were painted in faded letters on the side. We put on our white jumpsuits and climbed in carefully, stepping around the pelican crates already on board. Then Mr Hauser fired up the motor and manoeuvred us away from the shore.

Soon we were putting slowly along in the water, holding our nets.

"We're going so slowly," Olivia muttered to me. "Wouldn't we save more birds if we went a bit faster?"

Mr Hauser overheard. "That's because we're looking for the birds. We don't want to see one and zoom right past it."

I nodded. That made sense. We scanned the water for pelicans and, within five minutes, we saw one.

"There!" I pointed. A large pelican, coated with oil, was bobbing on the surface of the water.

"OK, I'll manoeuvre the boat closer, and you reach out and drop the net over his head," Mr Hauser told us. "Don't worry, it won't hurt him. He can't go very far, as he can't fly. We'll guide him closer to the boat and bring him aboard."

Mr Hauser carefully motored the boat closer to the pelican. I leaned over the edge, holding the long-handled net. The metal dug into my stomach a bit, but, holding my breath, I managed to drop the net down on the pelican. He only thrashed a bit, which told me how sick he was.

"Great work!" Mr Hauser said. He let the boat idle and reached over the edge. Together he and Olivia managed to haul the pelican up and bundle him into a crate.

"I know you're scared," Olivia said to the bird, trying to soothe it through the metal bars of the door. "But you're going to feel a lot better soon. Trust us."

We pulled two more pelicans from the water, both coated with oil. Mr Hauser had just manoeuvred the boat back to the beach when we saw a bird standing in the surf, looking around as if he couldn't quite believe where he was.

"Aha!" Mr Hauser said. "Let's pick up this guy. Our workers said they thought they'd got all the oiled birds off the beach itself, but they must have missed him."

I handed Olivia the net so she could have a turn, and she hurried forward as Mr Hauser instructed, holding the net up as if she were catching a butterfly. The move never would have worked with a healthy bird – it would have flown away immediately.

This pelican did spread his wings and try to fly away, but covered in oil, he was stuck. All he could do was run down the beach. Pelicans don't run quickly, even when they're healthy, though, so Olivia easily trapped him with the net. Mr. Hauser and I ran forward with the empty crate.

Bouncing around in the front seat of the van on the way home, I couldn't get the sight of the ruined beach out of my mind. Coastal Oil should have been out there cleaning up, and they weren't. Someone needed to *do* something.

I looked in the back of the van, where the birds were relatively quiet, clearly too sick to make any real noise. Then I looked over at Olivia. *We* needed to do something. I wasn't sure what yet.

But I was going to think of something.

Chapter 6

"OK, we have to think," I said to Olivia for what felt like the tenth time. We were sitting in my room, cross-legged on the bed, paper and pens at the ready. "We need to get Coastal Oil to take responsibility and clean up the spill. But they don't seem to care."

"And it's not that they don't *know* what's happening with the oil," Olivia said, gnawing at the end of her pen. "Mr Hauser said they do know.

So I don't think *telling* them what's happening is the answer."

"Besides, why would they listen to a couple of kids when they won't listen to the authorities?" I flopped back on the bed and stared at the ceiling, studying the poster of a group of kids clustered around a dolphin that I'd taped up there a few months ago. Suddenly it hit me. "That's it! Kids!"

Olivia looked startled. "Yeah, I know we're kids," she said carefully, as if I'd gone insane.

"No! We *need* kids!" I was so excited I leapt off the bed and almost launched myself into the wall by accident. "We can get a whole load to come out and clean up the beach with us. And we'll ask the media to come and do an article on us. We'll be cleaning up the beach, and we'll put pressure on Coastal Oil at the same time. Maybe they'll be so embarrassed that a group of kids are cleaning up *their* mess that they'll actually do something."

Olivia nodded thoughtfully. "That's a good idea. But how are we going to get the word out about the clean-up?" The words were barely out of her mouth before she snapped her fingers. "Wait, don't answer that." She opened her laptop and clicked around for a minute. Then she turned the screen towards me.

South Carolina Students' Environmental Action Network, the heading on the screen read. I scanned the page. It was a social media group. The news feed was filled with loads of comments and posts. The last one, about a road across a coyote habitat, was just a few minutes old.

"'Speak truth to power. Let your voice be heard. Stand up for South Carolina's natural environment, whether you're eight or eighteen'," I said, reading the group's mission statement aloud. "This is perfect!"

"The group has more than three thousand

members," Olivia said. She jabbed her finger at the screen. "If we put the word out here, people will see how horrible it is. We can document Pellie and take pictures of the beach. And we can call out Coastal Oil by name *and* tag local news stations. That way it'll show up on their feeds."

"And when we have enough interest, we'll put the word out about the clean-up day," I said. "You're brilliant!"

"OK, first of all, when are we doing this?" Olivia asked, grabbing her notebook.

"Saturday?" I suggested. "Does that work? Kids will be free at the weekend. It's only two days away, but we have to get out there. Every day the oil sits, it's poisoning more plants and animals."

"Agreed," Olivia said. "Saturday it is. What should we tell people to bring? What's our method going to be?" She poised her pen.

I frowned. "I think we need Mr Hauser for this one."

We found him in the office, the landline pressed to one ear, a pile of papers on his lap and a mobile phone dinging in front of him. But when he saw us, he paused. "What's up, girls?" he asked.

Briefly, we explained our clean-up plan – or what we had of it so far.

"Lead a clean-up yourselves?" Mr Hauser nodded. "I like how you think, girls."

"We need a couple of things from you," I said. "Can you help us come up with the clean-up method? Like tell us what equipment we'd need? And can you supervise on Saturday?"

Mr Hauser grinned. "Yes and yes. First of all, the method." He thought for a minute. "There's a lot of ways to clean up an oil spill, but because you guys want to do this on your own, we'd better go basic: shovels and rubbish bags. That works just as well as some of the more high-tech solutions, anyway. Here, write down these things."

I grabbed a blank intake form from the desk and turned it over.

"Fifty shovels, fifty rakes, five hundred industrial-strength rubbish bags, rubber gloves and overalls," Mr Hauser dictated. "Oh, and two big cases of granola bars and water. Ask people to bring their own boots, hand sanitizer and lunches. I'll get the rest of the supplies from my department."

"Let's do it!" Olivia shot out of her chair as if it had been rigged with an ejector seat.

We spent the next few hours running around the sanctuary, taking pictures of everything we thought people might be interested in: volunteers lifting soapy birds from the baths, the oiled birds in their cages, the clean birds and even the pile of birds that hadn't survived the spill.

I had to force myself to photograph the dead pelicans, lying with their beaks ajar and their eyes sunken and shrivelled. It broke my heart, but that was reality. People needed to see it.

Then we convinced Dad to give us a lift out to the beach, where he was going to check water levels. As we drove, Olivia and I brought him up to date on the action plan. He pledged his full support.

"Your mum and I will be happy to donate the water and granola bars," he offered. "I'll pick that stuff up this afternoon."

Out at the beach, we photographed as much of the stringy, tarry muck as we could, then moved on to the oily, brown-tinged water lapping at the sand. Olivia volunteered to stand in the gross water, and I photographed her legs to show how the oil was coating everything.

"Got everything you need, girls?" Dad called.

We nodded and ran towards the truck. As Dad guided it over the rough beach road, heading back to the sanctuary, he said, "Can I just say how proud I am of you girls for taking the initiative? You've really taken this crisis into your own hands. Some people think that because you're kids, you can't produce any kind of change. But that's not right. Kids can have a huge influence on real-world problems. They just need to gather and organize. And that's exactly what you're doing."

His words spread through me, warming me like Mr Hauser's sassafras tea had. "Thanks, Dad." I squeezed his rough hand where it lay on the gearstick.

"And I'm going to do my part too," he continued. "After I drop you girls at home, I'm heading to the shops to get the rest of the things you need."

Olivia and I jumped down from the truck and waved as he drove off. "Love you, Dad!" I shouted after him. He beeped the truck horn in response.

We wandered towards the pens, brainstorming what to write for our first Environmental Action Network post, when we almost bumped into Katie. She had a bucket in her hand and a grim look on her face.

"Hi, Katie! What's wrong?" I asked.

She looked down, as if she didn't want to say. "Hi, girls. I was almost hoping I wouldn't see you, so I wouldn't have to tell you the bad news."

Fear gripped my heart. "Oh, no. What?"

"I'm afraid Pellie isn't eating. We've tried dead fish, live fish, all types. He ignores them all," she said.

"Oh," Olivia said faintly. "That's not good."

"No, it's not." Katie spoke briskly now. "He may have swallowed more oil than we thought, in which case, he can't recover. But we'll see." Her voice caught as if she were going to cry. She turned and walked away abruptly, leaving us standing in the path.

Olivia and I exchanged a glance, then ran towards Pellie's pen and pressed our faces to the chain-link. He was there, standing calmly on the Astroturf-covered edge of his pool. Two other pelicans were waddling around, and one was in the water.

Pellie looked perfectly normal except for the fact that he wasn't moving as much as the others. He wasn't moving at all, I realized after a minute. He just stood still and blinked at us.

"He looks OK," Olivia said. She glanced around nervously. "I think we're supposed to be behind the curtain."

"Just one more minute." I stared at Pellie as if he could give me some answers. "Why won't you eat, boy?" I asked him. "Please eat! You can't be released until you can eat." That's what I wanted most for Pellie: to be free, flying above the water, not trapped in a cage surrounded by cement and fake grass.

Olivia and I stared at Pellie a long time, but he remained still. Only his eyes blinked, and occasionally he would slowly bob his head up and down.

Finally Olivia drew away from the chain-link. "This is hard to say, but there's nothing we can do for Pellie. Not right now. Either he's going to get better or he isn't."

Hearing that, I couldn't help letting out a little sob.

She put her arm around my shoulders. "You know what we *can* do? Help all those other birds and animals floating around in that oily water at the beach. There's still time to save them. So let's get started on those posts."

I nodded and wiped my eyes. "You're right. If we can't save Pellie, we can at least save some of his buddies. Let's go."

⚮

I could barely sit through dinner. Roast chicken had never seemed so boring. I was dying to get back upstairs and check on the response to our Sullivan's Beach Coastal Oil-Spill Clean-up. Olivia and I had just posted our photos and the clean-up info on the group's feed when Mum called me down to dinner and sent Olivia home to have dinner with Abby.

I fidgeted and pushed broccoli around on my plate until Mum announced dessert and brought out dishes of tinned peaches. "Can I be excused?" I asked.

"Of course, if you don't want any—"

But I already had my chair pushed back and was

halfway to the stairs. I took the steps two at a time and launched myself across my room to grab my laptop.

I flipped the computer open, hit refresh on the internet browser, and stared hungrily at the screen as the page loaded. Two hundred likes! Fifty comments! I scrolled down rapidly, reading as I went:

Anonymous 2 minutes ago
I'm totally grossed out by this disgusting act by Coastal Oil, and I will gladly be there on Saturday to clean up the beach.

Road_warrior721 5 minutes ago
I'll be there on Saturday, and I'll be bringing my cycling club for extra hands.

Coastal_Crew 12 minutes ago
Coastal Oil, are you out there? We're cleaning up your mess.

And, best of all:

Z.Davis_KQTD 30 minutes ago

Hi, Elsa and Olivia. I'm Zannie Davis with KQTD TV. I'd like to bring a camera crew out to film your clean-up day and interview you, if that's OK.

It was working! I immediately called Olivia. "Have you seen the post yet?" I asked as soon as she picked up.

"Not yet, we've just finished eating. Any word from Coastal Oil? We did tag them, so they should have seen it."

"Nothing. Radio silence from them, but we've got some amazing responses from everyone else," I said.

Olivia sighed. "Maybe they just need more shaming – oops, I mean time. In the meantime, what do we need for the clean-up?"

We spent the next half an hour planning, and by the time we'd hung up, I had a list of at least twenty things we needed. Saturday was just two days away. The beach was covered with oil. Pellie was sick. We were taking on a multi-national oil company and organizing an event for what could be hundreds of people.

But I didn't feel scared. For the first time since the spill, I felt hopeful.

Chapter 7

Saturday was clear and sunny – a rare Charleston day without humidity. The palmetto trees whipped in the brisk wind as Olivia and I sat in the cab of Mr Hauser's truck, leading the caravan of cars from Seaside Sanctuary out to Sullivan's Beach.

Mum and Dad had to stay behind at the sanctuary to oversee the washing tents, but Mr Hauser had promised to take good care of us all.

In the truck bed behind us were boxes and crates filled with all the supplies we'd need to salvage the shoreline.

"What if no one comes?" Olivia murmured next to me. "Just us. That's it."

I punched her gently in the arm. "Stop. We got like one million responses."

"That was yesterday. People forget. People flake out!" Her voice rose.

"They're not going to forget!" I insisted.

Olivia and I leaned forward as we approached the turn-off for the beach road, and I sucked in my breath. The road was lined with cars and trucks, all pulled over on the shoulder, almost bumper to bumper. Car doors slammed, one after another, as kids jumped out, carrying lunchboxes and gloves and wearing hats and old ragged shorts.

"People came!" Olivia breathed, her face bright with relief.

I laughed. "I told you they would."

Mr Hauser manoeuvred carefully down the road to the beach and parked. I jumped out and climbed into the bed of the truck. "Hey, everyone!" I shouted.

The kids started gathering round.

"What are you doing?" Olivia hissed. Her cheeks were red. She hated talking in front of people.

"Welcoming everyone!" I said loudly. Then I murmured to Olivia, "Just stand next to me. You don't have to say anything." I waved my arms to get everyone's attention. "I'm Elsa Roth from Seaside Sanctuary!" I shouted so the group could hear me over the waves and the breeze. "My friend Olivia and I are the ones who posted about the clean-up. Thank you all for coming!"

There was scattered applause, and someone cheered.

"Mr Hauser from the Department of Wildlife and Fisheries is here, and he's going to tell us the plan for today." I waved to Mr Hauser, who climbed up on the truck bed beside me.

"Everyone, my name is Chris Hauser, and I'm a wildlife biologist with the state of South Carolina," he said. "We have an important task ahead of us today – cleaning this beach. There are a lot of ways to clean up an oil spill, but we're going to be using the old-fashioned method: shovels and rubbish bags. It's important to keep your bodies and hands covered when you're securing the contaminated sand in the bags. This is untreated crude oil. You don't want it on your skin any more than a marine animal does."

Around me I could see the volunteers nodding. "Please put overalls and gloves on as soon as you're given them," Mr Hauser finished. "Let's get started!"

The group cheered, and I felt a thrill run through me. We were doing this!

We jumped down from the truck bed. "Lay the tools out in clean sand in rows," Mr Hauser said.

"Need help?" a tall boy with wavy brown hair asked. I nodded, and soon an eager crowd was gathered around us, handing out supplies.

Mr Hauser handed several rolls of string and a handful of stakes to two girls. "I'll help you two divide off sections of the beach with this string," he said. "That will help us keep track of the area we need to clean. And, Olivia, can you and two others be in charge of the water and refreshment area? Please, everyone, wash your hands with the water we've brought and use hand sanitizer before you eat or drink."

At least fifty kids started climbing into the crackly white overalls. "This is so disgusting," a girl with freckles said beside me. She grimaced, looking at the oil-strewn sand.

"That's what we thought," I said.

"I'm Norah, by the way. From the South Carolina Students' Environmental Action Network. I started the group." She shook my hand. "I'm so glad you organized this. We had no idea it was so bad."

"Are all these kids part of your group?" I asked her, gesturing at the kids suiting up all around us.

Norah nodded. "Yeah. We all wanted to come and help when we saw your posts. And I was really glad to see you tagged Coastal Oil and the local news. We always try to get exposure for the events we do. It makes more people aware of what's going on."

"There's no one from Coastal Oil here now," I said. "But a reporter, Zannie Davis, asked if she could come. I can't see any news trucks yet, though."

"She might turn up later. That would be really helpful," Norah replied.

Everyone got to work, and soon I was shovelling steadily near the tide line with a small group of volunteers, including the wavy-haired boy who'd first spoken to us. Each shovel of black sand I emptied into the rubbish bag beside me, revealing white sand underneath, felt like a victory. It was like I was personally healing a tiny section of beach.

I noticed the wavy-haired boy was struggling to tie up his rubbish bag. It was so full, the handles kept sliding out of his hands. "Hey, let me help you," I said. I held the top steady while he tied it up.

"Thanks." He wiped his oily glove on the seat of his overall and held it out. "Tom Bartel."

"Elsa Roth." I shook his hand with my rubber glove, which made us both laugh.

"How long have you been with this group?" I asked, helping him lift the heavy bag. We staggered towards the truck, where a pile was slowly building.

"Ah . . . here." He grabbed the bag from me and manhandled it on to the pile. He didn't answer my question. Maybe he hadn't heard me?

"It's really nice of your group to come out all together like this," I said, trying again as we made our way back to the shoreline. Side by side, we started shovelling up more dirty sand.

"Yeah. I-I mean, we . . . really wanted to. We feel responsible, you know?"

I glanced over at Tom. His cheeks were pink, and he was shovelling the sand into a bag with a little more concentration than was necessary. Was I missing something?

"Elsa! Olivia!" I looked up and saw Mr Hauser waving me over. He was standing beside a dark-haired woman and a guy with a baseball cap and a big camera on his shoulder.

Zannie Davis! I recognized her. I'd forgotten all about the news crew.

"Hello, girls," Zannie greeted us as Olivia and I both trotted over. "This is quite a clean-up effort you've organized." She was wearing more make-up than I'd ever seen in real life before, but I thought this was probably because of the camera. "Would you mind if we asked you a few questions on tape?"

"Not at all," I said. I tried to wipe off my rubber gloves, wondering how a white overall shaped like a bin bag would look on camera. I didn't even have to look at Olivia to know that she would be trying to hide behind me. Interviews really weren't her thing.

The cameraman turned on his camera and adjusted it, then Zannie asked us a lot of questions, like where we lived, how we found out about the oil spill, how Mr Hauser was helping us and why we decided to clean up the beach.

"Elsa, except for one person, everyone on this beach is a kid," Zannie said. She was using that buddy-buddy voice you hear on television. "What does it say that kids are cleaning up Coastal Oil's mess? If you had to send a message to Coastal Oil, what would you say to them?" She positioned the microphone in front of my face.

I leaned over and spoke carefully. I wasn't sure if I should be talking right into the camera or not. "We want to tell Coastal Oil that people should clean up their own messes. The animals and plants were just minding their own business on this beach, and now they're dying. Coastal Oil should be ashamed that they left the clean-up of this environmental disaster to kids." I looked at Zannie Davis. "How was that?"

She grinned. "Fantastic. You can look for the segment tonight on the six o'clock news and on our website. We'll also post it to all the social media sites where we have accounts." She frowned over my shoulder. "Is that—? Do you know that boy's name?"

I turned to see Tom Bartel loading another bag a few metres away. "Um, yeah. That's Tom Bartel. I think he's part of the Action Network."

The newswoman's eyebrows shot up. "He's a lot more than that. The Bartel family owns Coastal Oil. Tom is their only son."

My mouth dropped open. Olivia and I stared at each other. Someone from Coastal Oil *had* turned up. Just not who – or how – we'd expected.

"Zannie? Can you look at this tape?" the cameraman said, and the reporter turned away.

I nodded to Olivia. We made our way over to Tom, who was standing against the side of the truck, wiping sweat from his forehead. His face and overall were streaked with oil and grime. I could see the fatigue on his face.

"Why didn't you tell us your family owns Coastal Oil?" I asked. No point in beating around the bush.

Tom looked up, his eyes wide and startled. "I—um, sorry. Do you want me to leave?"

"No!" Olivia said. "Don't leave. We're just surprised, that's all. The reporter told us who your family is." She paused. "If you don't mind me asking, um, why are you here?"

"You have to admit, it's kind of weird," I added, my fists on my hips. "Your family's company clearly isn't willing to clean up the mess they've made." I waved my hand at the contaminated beach.

"I know." That was all Tom said, but he looked so destroyed, standing there covered in oil, that the anger I was feeling melted out of me. "It's my father. He thinks it's no big deal. I've tried to talk to him, but he doesn't listen. I wanted to do *something*. So when I saw the post, I came out."

"That was pretty brave," Olivia said quietly.

Tom shuffled his feet. "Not really. Not like what you guys have done."

Suddenly there was a commotion over by the trucks. We glanced over to see Zannie Davis and Mr Hauser standing toe to toe. He wasn't quite holding her back but almost.

"Well, I'm going to interview him!" Zannie Davis was saying. Her words carried on the ocean breeze. "What is he doing here?"

"Please leave him alone," Mr Hauser pleaded. "He's here because he cares, no matter what his family thinks. I'll give you whatever interview you need."

Eventually Zannie subsided, and we turned back to Tom.

"I'll talk to her," he said. "I don't care what my parents say." He started to march over to the camera.

"Wait!" I reached out and grabbed the sleeve of his overall to stop him. "I have a better idea. Don't make your parents angry by talking to the media. It would be way more useful if you talked to your parents about contributing money to the clean-up. Maybe once you tell them what happened today – and that the media was here – they'll listen to you."

Tom listened and then nodded slowly. "OK. I'll try again tonight. My dad will be home after eight o'clock." He took a deep breath and looked from Olivia to me to the beach and back again. "It's the least I can do."

Chapter 8

"Mum!" I shouted as Olivia and I tumbled out of the truck back at Seaside Sanctuary. "Abby!"

They ran out of the office, looking alarmed. "What's wrong?" Mum called.

"Everything's fine, no, it's not that," I panted. As fast as we could, our words tumbling over each other, Olivia and I explained what we'd started calling "The Strange Appearance of Tom Bartel".

Mum and Abby looked at each other, listening until we'd finished. I could see their brows furrowed, even in the setting sun.

"Do you think it will work?" I asked. "If he talks to his dad again?"

Mum sighed. "I don't know. It does sound like he feels bad about his family's role in the spill. And he did come to the clean-up."

Olivia nodded. "I don't blame him for not wanting to brag about who his family is. I'd be ashamed to show my face if *my* family was Coastal Oil. I'm just grateful he came to help anyway."

I nodded in agreement. "Let's check on Pellic before it gets dark."

We hurried towards the bird pens and skidded to a halt at Pellie's. The door was open, and the white curtain pushed aside. Olivia and I peeked past the curtain. The inside of the pen had a desolate look. There were no pelicans bobbing in the water, and the food dish was overturned on the floor.

Olivia and I looked at each other. I was afraid to see the truth in her face. "Maybe they released them early," I said hopefully.

"Maybe," Olivia echoed, but her voice sounded hollow.

My stomach was heavy, as if it was filled with rocks. Then footsteps crunched down the walkway, and Katie appeared. She was carrying a bucket of soapy water and a mop. She stopped when she saw us, putting the bucket down by the pen door and leaning the mop against the outside.

I knew she was about to speak, and I knew what she was going to tell us, but I didn't want to hear it. I wanted to press my hands over my ears and sing loudly, the way I used to when I was little.

"Girls, I'm so sorry," she said. "I'm sorry you had to find out this way. It happened very quickly. There was nothing we could do."

"No, no, no!" I cried out.

"I'm sorry," Katie repeated. "This is always the hard part of spills. You get attached. It's impossible not to."

Olivia stood at my side, taking deep, careful breaths, as if she was steadying herself. "Can we see him?" she asked faintly.

Katie gave us a long look, then nodded slowly. "If you're sure."

She went over to a wheelbarrow parked beside the pen that I hadn't noticed earlier. It was covered with one of the white curtains that hung in front of the pen. She pulled the curtain back to reveal three dead pelicans.

I recognized Pellie on top immediately. His bright eye was already sunken and cloudy.

His cleaned feathers were in disarray, and his beak hung open. I'd never seen anything look as dead as he did.

Olivia and I looked for a long time, not saying anything. Then I put my hand out and caressed Pellie's beak. Olivia stroked the soft feathers on his head. Then we stood back and watched Katie replace the sheet. There was nothing else we could do.

"There are always some like this," Katie said softly. "They seem to be recovering, but their systems are too damaged. They can't recover from the shock. I've been working these spills for years, but that part never gets any easier."

"He should have just died on the beach!" Olivia burst out. Her face was red and clenched. "He should have just died . . ." Her voice disappeared in a storm of sobs. She sank onto the ground and lowered her head into her hands.

"That's not true!" I knelt down, trying to see my friend's face. "At least here he had a chance. He could be clean and swim in his pool with the others."

Sadness seized my heart as I spoke. It wasn't enough. I knew that. Pellie should have lived. He'd never skim above the surface of the water now, diving for fish, bobbing on the waves.

"We did the best we could," I said sadly.

"That's right," Katie said. She helped Olivia to her feet and put an arm around each of us. "We did. We can't just abandon these animals, no matter how sick they are. We have to try with every single one."

Olivia nodded and wiped her eyes. "I know. I didn't mean what I said about leaving him on the beach."

"I know you didn't," Katie said. "Come on, girls. Work is the best medicine. Ten birds are waiting to be washed."

Olivia and I looked at each other and quickened our steps up the path. Pellie was dead. Nothing could change that. But these birds weren't. And we were going to do our best to save them.

❧

"Let's go and check out the KQTD website," I said, wiping my hands on a towel. It was nine o'clock, and we had finished with the birds. I was nowhere near ready for bed, though. Olivia and I hurried from the washing tent up to my room and opened my laptop.

Olivia rapidly navigated to the news channel's website. "Here it is!"

We both scooted close to the screen. There was Zannie Davis with a microphone in front of her mouth. Mr Hauser's truck was in the background.

"The Coastal Oil spill on Sullivan's Island has been called the worst South Carolina environmental disaster in ten years," Zannie said. "Five kilometres of beach is coated with oil. And who is cleaning it up? Local children."

The camera cut to a shot of all the volunteers in our white overalls, shovelling sand into rubbish bags. "There's me!" I pointed to the end. "Next to Tom."

"Darn, I'm over by the granola bars. I suppose she didn't film that," Olivia said.

Zannie Davis was still talking. "The children have just one message for Coastal Oil: Are you out there? We're cleaning up your mess. For KQTD, I'm Zannie Davis."

The video ended. We sat for a minute, staring at the screen. "Well, what now?" Olivia said, just as my phone rang.

"Elsa?" a voice said when I answered.

"Yeah?"

"This is Tom," the caller said. "Tom Bartel."

"Oh, Tom!" I'd given him my phone number at the clean-up, but I was still a bit surprised to hear from him. I hit the speaker button, so Olivia could hear too.

"Listen, I've got some news." Tom's voice was excited, as if he couldn't get the words out fast enough. "I talked to my dad again tonight. I told him about the clean-up and all the kids who turned up. He saw the news story, and then his work phone started just blowing up with calls! He had an emergency meeting with his board on conference call. They're fully committing to the clean-up! There's going to be a press conference in the morning announcing that Coastal Oil will supply one-hundred per cent of the funds to remove the oil and wash the animals. Plus three hundred more volunteers!"

"Wow! That's — just wow!" I wished I could think of something more to say, but I was too happy.

"Whoo!" Olivia did a happy dance around my room. "We did it!"

"You really did." I couldn't see Tom, but I could tell he was smiling.

"You did too, Tom," I said. "You stood with us. You turned up to help. You convinced your dad to help. And together, we changed things."

"That's right," Tom said. "We did it together."

Epilogue

"Wake up, honey." Mum shook my shoulder in the darkness. I blinked up at her, then fumbled for my jeans and sweatshirt. It was one o'clock in the morning, and Olivia and I were going with Mr Hauser to release the pelicans.

The oil spill was over. At least, Seaside Sanctuary's part in it was over. Coastal Oil had come through with money and volunteers, and bird-cleaning operations were being transferred to a big facility further up the coast.

The temporary buildings at Seaside Sanctuary had been taken down. The bird pens had been dismantled and driven away in trucks. The beach – well, it was as clean as it was going to get. Not the same as it was, but better than it had been.

But for the pelicans, the story wasn't

quite over. They had one last part to play. And so did we.

Out in the pitch-black night, I found my way to the big van where Mr Hauser was loading the last pelican crates. Olivia was already in the front seat, looking as sleepy as I felt.

"Glad you girls could get up," Mr Hauser said, slamming the van doors and coming around to the front. "We've got a few hours' drive. The pelicans need to be released early so they have plenty of time to acclimate themselves before nightfall."

"We're glad to," I managed to get out before an enormous yawn took over.

"Hey!" a voice said. I turned and saw a tall figure emerging from the darkness.

"Tom!" I said, recognizing him as he drew closer.

"Room for one more?" he asked.

"Absolutely!" Olivia shoved over on the seat.

Mr Hauser grinned at us. "I didn't think you girls would mind if our friend here joined us."

"Oh no, you were right!" I assured him. "Tom deserves to be here to see the release. This is as much his victory as it is ours."

"I thought so too," Mr Hauser said. He started the ignition and pulled out of the car park. We all waved goodbye to my parents. "Let's get on the road."

❦

Three dark and sleepy hours later, we bumped to a halt along a lonely beach road. Jumping out, we opened the van doors and pulled out the crates, lining them up along the beach facing the ocean. The sky was dark grey in the west, but in the east, a pale pink glow was starting to spread across the horizon.

"OK, when I say, start opening the doors,"

Mr Hauser told us. "Just go along the row. The pelicans will come out on their own. After that, it's up to them." He paused for a moment. "Now!"

Tom, Olivia and I hurried along the row of crates, swinging the doors open. Then we stood back and watched. One by one, the pelicans waddled out, blinking in the growing light. Some stood quietly on the beach. Others waded into the surf. Then one spread his wings and flapped.

"Look!" I cried.

The bird flapped his wings again and then, as I held my breath, he soared up and away, skimming along the surface of the grey water. Another followed and another. Soon the air in front of us was full of pelicans wheeling and flapping above the ocean.

"They're back!" I said. "Back where they should be."

"And let's hope they can continue to fly here,"

Mr Hauser said. "Thanks to all of you, they have a better chance."

About the author

Emma Carlson Berne is the author of many books for children and young adults. She loves writing about history, plants and animals, outdoor adventures and sport. Emma lives in Ohio, USA, with her husband and three little boys. When she's not writing, Emma likes to ride horses, hike and read books to her sons.

About the illustrator

Erwin Madrid grew up in California, USA, and earned his BFA in Illustration from the Academy of Art College in San Francisco. During his final year, Erwin was employed by PDI/DreamWorks Animation, where he contributed production art for *Shrek 2*. He later became a visual development artist for the Shrek franchise, the *Madagascar* sequel and *Megamind*. He has designed cover artwork for children's books for publishers including Harper Collins, Random House and Simon and Schuster.

Glossary

acclimate adapt to a new climate, environment or situation

crisis situation that has become very serious

desolate lacking signs of life

ecosystem plants and animals living in a particular area and the relationship between them and their surroundings

initiative first step or movement

poise carrying and presenting yourself with confidence

preen when a bird cleans its feathers with its bill

salvage rescue or save, especially from wreckage or ruin

Talk about it

1. The oil spill badly affects the Charleston area.
    How would you feel if your town had an oil
    spill that hurt the wildlife? What would you
    do to help out?

2. While cleaning the pelicans, Mr Hauser tells
    Elsa and Olivia that it's important to make
    sure the pelicans are a little afraid of humans.
    Talk about why that is important to help the
    pelicans.

3. Elsa notices that the pelicans that were hurt
    by the oil are visibly different when the
    Seaside Sanctuary team helps get them into
    the rescue centre. What are some of the
    signs she sees that the birds aren't behaving
    normally because of the oil?

Write about it

1. Elsa and Olivia care deeply about all the pelicans, but they grow very attached to one in particular. Would it be difficult for you to not treat the pelicans as pets? Write a few sentences explaining why or why not.

2. After Elsa and Olivia post online asking for help, one of the people who joins the team is Tom Bartel. Why do you think he came to the clean-up? Write a paragraph from Tom's perspective explaining why he came to the beach.

3. Imagine you are Elsa. Write your own version of the post asking for anyone to help clean up the oil spill, describing the state of the beach and what has happened to the pelicans.

More about pelicans

Pelicans are very recognizable birds, especially because of the pouches on their throats. Did you know that pelicans use their throat pouches to catch fish and to carry materials for building their nests? Here are ten more facts that might surprise you:

1. All kinds of pelicans have a throat pouch. Their pouches can hold more than their stomachs.

2. Pelicans can have a wingspan up to three metres wide. They can have trouble getting into the air because of their size, but with the right gust of wind they can fly high into the sky.

3. Pelicans are very quiet when they're away from their breeding colony or when it's not time for food.

4. Pelicans live on most of the continents in the world. The only continent pelicans don't live on is Antarctica.

5. There are eight different species of pelican. The pelican with the largest bill size is the Australian pelican, which can have a bill as long as 50 centimetres!

6. Pelicans are one of the few bird types that breathe through their mouths instead of their nostrils.

7. In the wild, pelicans can live for up to 25 years. In captivity, they can live for more than 50 years.

8. Pelicans mostly eat fish, and they can eat as much as two kilograms of fish a day. Brown pelicans dive under the water to catch fish, while other pelicans keep their heads above water.

9. A pelican can't swallow fish until it drains the water it scooped up out of its pouch. A pelican's throat pouch can hold eleven litres of water.

10. Pelican feathers are waterproof, but only when tiny parts of each feather called barbs lock together. Pelicans and other birds are in danger during an oil spill, as the oil separates the barbs and exposes the birds to the cold.

Seaside SANCTUARY

When 12-year-old Elsa Roth's parents uproot their family and move them from Chicago, Illinois, to a seaside marine biology facility in Charleston, South Carolina, she expects to be lonely and bored. Little does she know that Seaside Sanctuary might just be the most interesting place she could have imagined. Whether she's exploring her new home, getting to know an amazing animal or basking in the sun, Elsa realizes there's fun to be had – and mysteries to be solved – at Seaside Sanctuary.

Read all of Elsa's seaside adventures!

Discover more amazing books
at:
www.raintree.co.uk.